PIPE DREAMS

PIPE DREAMS

Anne Schulman

BBC
LARGE
PRINT

First published in 2000 by
New Island
This Large Print edition published
2010 by BBC Audiobooks by
arrangement with
New Island

ISBN 978 1 405 62298 1

British Library Cataloguing in Publication Data available

Printed and bound in Great Britain by
CPI Antony Rowe, Chippenham and Eastbourne

CHAPTER ONE

Meany Freeney sat at the bar nursing his pint of Guinness. Of course, Meany was not his real name. He had been christened that in school when he refused to share a bar of chocolate. He had made it last for five whole days. The name stuck and he had been known as Meany ever since.

John Doyle stood quietly wiping a glass. In all his years at Doyle's pub he had never known Meany to order a pint. It was always a half. Nor had he ever seen him in the bar before seven in the evening.

'Everything all right, Meany?' he asked.

'No, not really,' Meany said with a sigh.

John waited. Something was going on, he was sure of it.

'Can I help?' John tried again after

a few minutes.

Meany shook his head.

John loved to be in the know. He hated to be kept in the dark. He felt it was his duty to be the first with any news. Good or bad.

Meany drained his glass and got down from the bar stool. 'See you later, John,' he said and left without another word. Sharing a secret with John would be like telling the world.

Meany opened the door of his car and made sure that his seat was still safely tied in place. The Gardai had warned him that unless he got the seat fixed they would have to fine him. It was dangerous sliding around the way it did. But, Meany thought, taking it to a garage would cost money. He would find time some day soon and mend it himself. No point worrying about that now. He had more important things on his mind.

Meany drove along the narrow country roads towards the farm. The beauty of the trees with their fresh green leaves was lost on him. He saw only pound signs. He had no eyes for the baby lambs hopping and skipping alongside their mothers. The memory of his bank manager's smile blotted them from his mind. Even the soft, sweet smell of the late spring afternoon was wasted on him because the car window was stuck fast. His head was full of troubles. And of Julie.

Life had not been the same since Julie had come back to look after her Mam. Julie and Meany had grown up together. They had been in the same class at school. Made their confirmation together. Gone to the pictures and the same dances—but not together.

And when they were old enough, drank at Doyle's pub. Meany had always been shy. Far too shy to tell Julie that she was the prettiest girl he had ever seen. That was before she had gone to work in Dublin. Now she was beautiful. Masses of brown curls and big blue eyes. Even bluer now because of the eyeshadows she used.

The last three months had flown by. They had been the happiest of his life. He dashed through his work on the farm each day. He could not wait to get to Doyle's each evening. Julie always made a bee line for him when she came in. Her smile melted his heart. It made him the envy of all the other fellows. He had taken to sitting at a table now. It was easier to watch the door from there. Meany always waited until Julie arrived before he ordered his half-pint. After all, there were two drinks to be paid for now, his and hers. Some nights she had two drinks. Last Wednesday it was three, but Tom Scully had paid for the third. They usually gave Doyle's a miss on Mondays. They went to the cinema instead. Monday nights were half price.

'No point in paying double to see the same film,' Meany reasoned.

'Whatever you say,' Julie agreed.

Julie liked Meany a lot. An awful lot. He was not like most of the other guys she knew. They were full of smart remarks. Touching her up, pretending it was an accident. Meany was polite. Kind. Thoughtful. Certainly he was mean, she knew that. Everyone knew that. But it was one of his few faults and she was working on that.

CHAPTER TWO

'I can't stay long tonight,' Julie warned as she arrived at Doyle's, spot on seven o'clock.

'Is your Mam worse?' Meany asked as he pulled out a chair for her.

'She's been bad most of today. My sister is with her now. I didn't want to let you down. I'll just have one drink, then I must get back,' she said.

Before he had time to sit down, Julie threw back her gin and tonic in a couple of gulps and pushed back her chair.

'Sorry, Meany, I have to go,' she apologised.

Meany understood. 'Keep an eye on my glass, I'll be back in a minute,' he called to the barman.

He walked Julie to her car and waited until she was safely on her way.

Meany left a great wave of pity for her. It was a little over a year since his own Mam had died. He still missed her terribly. Especially on cold winter nights when the wind and rain howled round the farmhouse. They tapped on the windows and rattled the doors like a couple of playful children. It was lonely with only the fire and the crackling radio for company. He had almost owned a television once. He found it in a skip. But, after weeks of tinkering with it, he gave up and returned it to its resting place. The radio was just as good, he decided. And he loved reading. He liked true crime stories and books about farming. He was a regular at the library. A visit every three weeks without fail. His Mam had not approved of buying books. 'Why buy them when you can get them for free?' she used to say.

His Mam knew the value of money. She could make a pound stretch further than anyone else he knew. Take soap for instance. She kept all the ends, melted them down, then pressed them together to make a new bar. She was a whiz with an onion too. Used every scrap of it. Even the papery skin went into stews. No one could do more with the monthly Sunday roast than she could. Sliced and reheated with gravy on Monday. Served cold with boiled potatoes on Tuesday. Meat and potato rissoles on Wednesday and scraped to the bone with a salad on Thursday.

Now that he thought about it, he had never heard her grumble about cooking on the old turf-fired stove. She never minded giving the clothes a good scrub on the washboard. No new-fangled washing machines for her. Not like Julie, who said she would rather die than stand scrubbing collars with a bar of soap.

Meany knew all about Julie's Dublin apartment. If she needed heat she just flicked a switch. The same with the kettle. A jug-kettle, she called it. She had an iron that jetted out water at the touch of a button. And, if she was not in the humour to talk to someone, she let her answerphone take over.

'I couldn't live without all my mod cons,' she told Meany.

*   *   *

Meany walked slowly back to the table and picked up his drink.

'You're very quiet tonight, Meany. Has Julie dumped you?' Tom Scully called over from the bar, with a grin.

'Her Mam's bad,' Meany explained in his quiet, good-natured way.

Tom was always sniffing around Julie. Chatting her up. He fancied her like mad. She thought he was a bit of a poser. She'd come across enough of those in Dublin.

'So when's the big day then?' Tom jeered.

'What big day?' Meany asked

innocently.

'Come on, you know what I mean,' Tom laughed.

Meany frowned but ignored the question. It was naming the Big Day that was the cause of all his troubles. He thought of nothing else. Even in his sleep. And there had been precious little of that these past few weeks. Tom's teasing did not usually rattle him. But Meany was not in the mood for his nonsense tonight. He had a lot of thinking to do.

CHAPTER THREE

Meany filled the blackened kettle and put it on the stove to boil. He pushed the table to one side and moved the old threadbare rug out of the way. The screwdriver fitted neatly between the two floorboards. With a firm tug one of the boards swung upwards. He removed the bank books from their hiding place and spread them on the table. Then, before he made the tea, he checked that there were no gaps in the curtains.

Meany smiled as he turned the pages of his latest deposit book. He had been saving from the age of six. Even now, with interest rates at an all-time low, his cash was growing steadily. His heart raced as he saw the biggest amount of all, the payment from the sale of the five-acre plot next to Billy White's farm.

But his smile soon faded. The sight of the hefty sum brought a frown to Meany's brow. Billy had swindled his mother. Wiped her eye without so much as a blink. He begged her to sell him the land so that he could produce more crops. He had a growing family to raise.

'You're not growing crops on it. What use is it to you?' Billy asked.

He went on and on until finally she had given in. After all, it would bring a tidy sum for something they were not using anyway.

Exactly one month later Billy White sold the land to some property developers for double the price. When the news of the sale broke, in Doyle's pub, his Mam took to her bed for two days. She had never done that before. Not even when she was sick. When she finally came downstairs she told Meany that Billy White's name was never to be mentioned in her house again. And it never was.

Meany was not a poor man, far from it. His father had always been careful. His mother even more so. Even their savings and his own, Meany had a tidy cushion behind him. Apart from his bank manager, no one had any idea how much money he had. Plenty had tried to guess. Meany wished that the bank manager did not have to know either. His money was his affair, nobody else's. If it had not been for the fire which gutted a neighbour's farmhouse, Meany would never have talked his mother into using the bank in the first place. The farmer had not trusted banks one little bit and kept his life savings stashed all over the house.

But, that was then, and this was now. How much of his money would be left if he married Julie? She saw no sin in spending. She teased him about his meanness all the time. Everyone did. But let them, he didn't care.

CHAPTER FOUR

Meany stood behind Julie at the graveside. His heart ached for her. When she could bear no more, she turned to Meany and hid her face in his shoulder.

Meany stood silently as she leaned against him. The nearness of her curled through him. He could smell her perfume. And feel the softness of her curls on his face. A blush stained his cheeks. This was neither the time nor the place to feel the way he did.

Later, as people paid their respects to Julie and her sister, Meany waited quietly by the bay window of the cottage. Julie, her mother and her sister, Katie, had done a good job of restoring it. It looked different now. Bigger. Brighter. All white with just splashes of colour. A real picture-book cottage. Meany gazed through the window at the garden. What would happen to the cottage now? Julie and her sister both worked in Dublin. Would they sell the cottage, or keep it? But more importantly, would Julie return to Dublin and stay there if he didn't ask her to marry him? With her Mam gone and the cottage sold, Julie would have no reason to come back to Wexford.

Meany supposed that he and Julie had a kind of understanding. Nothing official. No engagement ring or anything. The thought of that made his blood run cold. The expense. God knows what a ring would cost. And then there was the farm. Julie would not live there as it was. She had thrown out enough hints about that. She had said so in lots of different ways. She was forever at him to modernise it. To have heating put in. Install a phone. Get a proper cooker and a washing machine. Buy comfortable furniture for himself. Clean up the garden. An endless stream of suggestions poured from those luscious, red lips.

'I'll probably go back to Dublin next week,' Julie told a neighbour. 'There's nothing to keep me here now, is there?'

Meany's hand shook. He wobbled the glass to his lips, his mind racing.

'Nothing to keep her here,' he muttered to himself. 'What about me?'

Julie smiled. She could see Meany's reflection in the window. She watched his hand shake. Her remark had scared him and she was glad. She knew how to push his buttons. Meany would not want to lose her, she was sure of that. He loved her, she knew that too. But he needed a push. He needed to make up his mind. A bit of a fright never hurt anyone.

'Are you OK, Meany?' she asked rubbing his arm fondly.

'I'm fine. How are you doing? Are you feeling better now?'

'I'll be all right once everybody has gone. People are very kind. They try to help by saying such nice things about Mam. But that only seems to make it harder. I suppose I'd be more upset if they said nothing,' Julie replied.

'I know what you mean. I felt the same way,' Meany agreed.

'Will you stay and have something to eat when everyone's gone?' Julie asked as someone else came up to talk to her.

'Of course I will,' Meany said. He wished he could give her a hug. But he couldn't. Not in front of all these people.

Meany poured another drop of whiskey into his glass. He rarely drank spirits but today was special. He returned to his place at the window. He needed two more days. Just two more days to make up his mind. As much as he loved Julie he had no intention of telling her about the two men who had been sniffing around his farm. Property developers who had discovered the ten-acre site which ran down to the sea. They had paid him two visits already and told him they would be back to make him an offer. This time there would be no mistake. This time he would get the full value of the land. Not like his poor Mam, diddled out of her rights. This plot was far bigger and better than the one she had sold to Billy White.

CHAPTER FIVE

'You couldn't find a better site for holiday homes. Not in this area,' his bank manager had pointed out. 'Where else would you find land leading directly onto the beach? Who else has farmland with a ready-made road running the length of it? I don't know of any around here. And best yet, all within easy reach of Dublin. You're on to a winner there, Meany.'

Meany remembered the bank manager's words as he sat rooted to his chair. He was frozen rigid. Frozen with shock, more like. When the developers made their offer they mistook his silence as a refusal. Within minutes they had upped the price.

Meany's brain finally engaged. He wondered if he tried to speak would real words come out of his mouth?

But, stunned though he was, Meany's mind was racing. He was nobody's fool. Without a single word from him the two men had increased the price. They must be mad keep to get their hands on the land. What if he held out for more? What if he told them that he'd had a better offer? That was done all the time. He had read about it.

'I'll have to think about this,' Meany said. 'I'm not in any hurry to sell. Prices are going up all the time. It would have to be well worth my while to part with the land just now. A few people have asked about it. It's a great site. Yes I'll think about it. I'll contact you tomorrow and give you my answer.'

The two men looked at each other. This quiet farmer was not the pushover they expected him to be. They believed him when he said that other developers were nosing about. Holiday homes were a licence to print money these days. The houses were sold straight off the plans. Of all the land they had seen this was far and away the best. They would have liked to have closed the deal there and then.

But Meany stood his ground. He hoped that they could not see his pulse beating wildly against the collar of his open-necked shirt. Another minute of this and he would need open-heart surgery.

As soon as they disappeared from sight, Meany ran to his car and slammed it into gear. The rope holding the seat snapped and almost sent him hurtling through the windscreen. As he retied the rope, Meany made himself a promise. If the developers increased their price he would take the car into the garage, have the seat repaired once and for all. If they *really* increased the price he would have the window done too.

Meany squealed to a halt outside his solicitor's office and dashed inside. Mark Austin saw him without an appointment. If Meany was wandering around at this time of day there had to be a good reason. If Meany was visiting his office at all there had to be a good reason. It did not happen often.

Meany told Mark about the events of the morning, then sat back and waited to hear what the solicitor had to say.

'Smart move, Meany. I couldn't have handled things better myself,' Mark said.

Meany breathed a sigh of relief. He was glad that Mark agreed.

'So where do we go from here?' Meany asked.

'We don't. We sit and wait. Let them come back to you,' Mark replied.

'But I promised them I would let them know tomorrow,' Meany explained.

'That's OK. Let them stew a while. I'm sure they will be back on your doorstep soon enough,' said Mark.

'How sure?' Meany asked.

'Positive,' Mark assured him.

'And what happens then?' Meany wanted to know.

'Wait a couple of days. Then phone them. Apologise. Say that you have been busy and that you meant to get in touch. Tell them that you are sorry to have to refuse their offer because you've had a better one. A much better one. They'll be expecting to pay more, believe me.' Mark watched Meany's face turn pale. 'You don't have to deal with them if you don't want to, Meany. I'll handle the sale for you if you like.'

Meany felt his stomach begin to churn. He was not into all this wheeling and dealing.

'What happens if they go somewhere else?' Meany asked.

Mark shrugged. 'Where? There's no better site on this part of the coast,' he said. 'Don't worry Meany. Developers are like buses, there'll be another one along in a minute.'

Meany was out of his depth. But he needed to make his mind up quickly. Another few days and Julie would be back in Dublin. She might meet someone else. She could be lost to him forever. He could not think straight. The solicitor glanced at his watch. 'Listen, Meany, I have an appointment in a couple of minutes. Why don't you go off and have a drink and a sandwich maybe? That will give you time to decide what you want to do.'

Meany began to head for Doyle's pub, then changed his mind. The last thing he needed just now was John Doyle and his questions. He crossed the road and walked in the opposite direction to another bar. It was still early and the bar was quiet. He sat at the counter and ordered a cup of tea and a cheese sandwich.

Two pounds seventy-five for a sandwich and a cup of tea! He thought he was going to choke. It would not cost more than twenty pence to make them at home. He was not interested in the barman's excuses. It was a disgraceful waste of money. But it was too late to send the sandwich back, he had already taken a bite out of it. He would not come here again in a hurry.

By three o'clock Meany was back at the farm. Mark Austin was handling the sale for him. The price would remain a secret between the buyers and himself. And Mark Austin too, unfortunately. The bank manager would also have to know.

On his way home Meany had popped into the cottage and invited Julie for supper. There was a bit of cold chicken left from the night before. He stopped at the bakery and bought two eclairs. Another scandal. Thirty-two pence for a cream cake. His Mam could have baked a whole batch for less. But he did not have time to worry about that now, he had to make up for being away most of the day. After that he would have to wash and then make supper.

Meany's heart lifted when he heard Julie's car. He rushed outside. He could see a bottle peeping out of the basket she was carrying.

'I brought some wine,' she said as she gave him a peck on the cheek. 'And some cold roast beef. My sister has gone back to Dublin and I'll never get through this on my own.'

Meany took the basket from her and followed her into the farmhouse.

'Ooh! Its dark in here,' she said with a shiver.

'I'll put the light on.' Meany reached for the switch. He was used to walking around by the light of the fire and often sat in the dark.

A big pot of potatoes was hissing and bubbling on the grid above the stove. There were none better, Meany always claimed. Home-grown and floury. He never tired of them. Julie's meat would go down a treat he thought as he put the chicken away for the following night. It was a bit scrawny he had to admit.

'How do you cook on that thing?' Julie asked as she watched him raking the fire to speed up the potatoes.

'I just do, I'm used to it,' Meany said giving the fire another poke.

'Let's open the wine while we're waiting,' Julie suggested. 'Where do you keep the glasses?'

'There, on the table.'

'No, the wine glasses, I mean.'

'I haven't any, they're the only ones I have.'

Julie recognised the glasses. They had been give-aways at all the garages a few years back. She poured the wine and carried the glasses over to the turf-fired stove. She lowered herself into the easy-chair and jumped up quickly as a broken spring attacked her skinny behind.

'Sorry, I forgot to warn you about the spring,' Meany apologised. 'I meant to fix it but haven't got round to it yet.'

'God, Meany! There's nothing left to fix. Why don't you sling it out and buy yourself a decent chair before you do yourself an injury? There's loads of space for furniture in here. The room could do with a lick of paint too. It's a pity that I'm not staying on, I could have done it for you,' she said cunningly.

Meany's heart dropped into his boots. 'You are going back then?' he asked.

'Why not? With Mam gone and my sister back in Dublin, I'd be lonely.'

'You have me,' Meany reminded her.

'I know I do. And I'm grateful for that. You've been wonderful. But I'd be lonely at the cottage all by myself.' Would he never take the hint? she wondered.

'The potatoes are done,' said Meany, quickly changing the subject.

The wine helped to ease his shyness and they chattered happily while they ate. Julie told him more about the pressures of her public relations job. How sometimes she wished that she could get away from the rat race.

Meany nodded. 'I'm glad I'm not part of it. Running the farm single-handed is pressure enough,' he said.

'Would you not get someone in to help you?' Julie asked.

'There's no need. I can manage on my own. I have a man who gives me a hand when I go to the market, otherwise everything's fine,' Meany explained.

'What about holidays? Does he take over then?'

Meany looked at her blankly. 'I've never had a holiday. I've never thought about one.'

'That's terrible, Meany. Everyone needs a holiday,' Julie said.

'Why?' Meany asked.

Julie's heart sank. Another problem that would need sorting.

'People need holidays. Everybody

needs a break now and then. It gets you away from your worries for one thing. Apart from that, it's nice to visit new places. See something of the world,' she explained.

'I like Wexford,' Meany said stubbornly.

He did not want to travel. He liked being at the farm. No crowds pushing and shoving, no traffic jams. No noise. Just the sound of the countryside. The song of the birds. Sheep bleating. The drone of a tractor. Familiar sounds. He had been to Dublin twice and could not wait to get back to the peace and quiet of the farm.

'I'll make some coffee,' Julie offered.

'I'm sorry . . . sorry,' Meany stammered. 'I don't have any. I forgot to buy it.'

Julie watched a blush rise to his cheeks and felt a great tug of love for the shy man. He looked like a lost, little boy.

Without any warning she heard herself say, 'Meany, are you going to ask me to marry you or do I have to propose to you?'

Now that the words were out, she sat back on her chair and waited.

'I was...I was going to ask you, Julie, really I was,' Meany stuttered. 'But now that you've brought it up: Will you marry me, Julie?'

'Of course I will!' She laughed. 'But on one condition, Meany, you have to fix up the farmhouse first. Make it a real home. I'll help you. We can do it together. We'll need central heating and a proper cooker. The place needs decorating and some decent furniture.'

Now that Julie's demands were out in the open, Meany's worst nightmare had come true. But also his wildest dreams.

CHAPTER SIX

Meany looked about the room. In the cold light of day it did not look too shabby. But, he had given Julie his word and he would not go back on it. As he sipped the strong tea, he began to make plans. He would go to the gas showrooms later and find out the cost of putting in heating. He could pick up a second-hand cooker in a local sale. There were often adverts in the paper. For furniture too. Julie had offered to take care of it all. But Meany knew that she would head straight for the most expensive shops. It would cost a fortune that way. No, he would do it himself. He'd wait until Julie went back to Dublin, then scout around. And then there was the ring. The thought of that sent the blood pounding round his head. He would have to buy Julie a ring. But he would choose that too. They had talked briefly about the wedding the previous night. She wanted a white wedding with all the trimmings, a reception at a nice hotel. Meany had been so dizzy with happiness that he had let her chatter on. He would be quite content with a church service then back to Doyle's pub for a drink. Maybe, if the land was sold, a few sandwiches too.

Later that afternoon Meany listened to what the gas salesman had to say. Not in a million years would he pay what they were asking. It would cost thousands to run a pipe from the main road to the farm. And that was just for starters. The pipes would need to be brought into the house. Walls drilled through, radiators fitted, mess everywhere.

'Forget it,' Meany said, 'I'll use electricity instead.'

'Suit yourself, that's up to you. But in the long run gas would be a lot cheaper,' the salesman said with a sniff.

He would say that, Meany thought. At this rate he'd be broke before he even took a step down the aisle. Julie had such big ideas. Well, she would have to forget about gas heating and cooking, it was not going to happen.

Meany was not looking forward to breaking the news to Julie. But he was determined not to part with that kind of money. No matter how much she wanted gas central heating.

'But, Meany, we don't want to be faced with huge electricity bills for the rest of our lives, do we?' Julie asked as she wrapped her arms round his neck and kissed him.

Meany felt himself weaken. She had a terrible effect on him.

'We wouldn't need heating all the time,' he said. 'Only if it was a very cold night. That way we could keep the stove. It has always heated the house up until now.'

'Does it heat the bedrooms?' Julie asked.

'No,' Meany admitted.

'There you are then,' Julie said.

'What about oil?' Meany asked.

'Sure, if you don't mind running out and then relying on deliveries in the middle of winter. Anyway, oil's even dearer,' she added, not at all sure of her facts.

'Why don't we just leave things the way they are for the moment. We can give the place a lick of paint, buy a new chair, then see how things go from there,' Meany suggested.

'Get real, Meany,' Julie snapped. 'This is the twenty-first century, not the Dark Ages. If you want to marry me, and want me to live here with you, you know what to do. If you don't, just say so. This conversation is a waste of time. I'm going home.'

Julie was furious. As she grabbed her bag from the easy-chair the strap caught on the broken spring. 'And throw that heap of junk you call a chair on the bonfire while you're at it,' she spat at him.

Before Meany had a chance to answer, his solicitor, Mark Austin, arrived. Julie nodded coldly to him as she flounced out of the farmhouse. Meany watched helplessly through the window as she slammed her car door and sped off down the road in a cloud of dust.

Meany listened to what Mark Austin had to say.

'That's fantastic,' Meany gasped as he heard the developers final take-it-or-leave-it offer. 'What did you tell them?'

'I told them I'd speak to you, then phone them back. I don't think you'll do better. Will you accept their offer?' Mark wanted to know.

'Yes, yes I will,' Meany replied. This could be his saviour.

*   *   *

Meany's car bumped and banged along the rough road leading to Julie's cottage.

41

'Don't give up on me now,' he pleaded aloud to the frail rope which was threatening to give way again. Julie had been so furious when she left the farm she might never speak to him again. Well, she could have her precious heating and her gas cooker now. And he would throw the chair out if it made her happy. Better still, he could put it in one of the sheds. It would be grand to sit in while he ate his lunch.

Meany breathed a sigh of relief. Julie's car was still outside the cottage.

'Its open,' she called in answer to his knock. 'I'm upstairs. Packing.'

'Where are you going?' Meany asked as he watched her throwing her clothes into a case.

'Back to Dublin.'

'Ah, Julie, don't be like that, I'm sorry, I didn't mean to upset you. You can have your heating, I promise,' he said.

'You said that last night, Meany,'

'I know I did, but I got a terrible shock when they told me the price,' Meany explained.

'What do you expect? The farm isn't exactly on the main road, is it? Or on the main gas supply for that matter either,' Julie said as she folded his favourite blue sweater and put it in the case. 'It's not going to work for us, Meany. I don't want to spend the rest of my life fighting and begging every time we need something. I can't live that way.'

'You won't have to, I promise,' Meany said. 'Please, Julie, stop packing. I'd do whatever you want.'

Julie looked into his pleading eyes. He was such a softie underneath all his meanness. He couldn't help it, she supposed. His mother had brought him up that way. She had turned meanness into a fine art.

'You'll put in gas heating?' she asked.

'I will,' Meany replied.

'And get rid of that old stove? Buy

a gas cooker?'

'Yes.'

'A *new* gas cooker?'

'A new gas cooker,' Meany repeated.

'And we'll do the place up? Paint it from head to toe?' Julie pressed.

'Whatever you say.' Meany felt like a drowning man.

'And we'll have a proper wedding?' Julie knew that this was the moment to iron things out. She might not get a chance like this again.

'Can't we talk about that later?' Meany asked. At this rate every penny he expected to make from the sale would be spent before it ever reached the bank.

'Now is as good a time as any,' Julie said firmly. 'I'll help with the wedding. Pay for the food. And the cake.'

Meany cheered up. All he would have to do was stand a round of drinks. That would not be too bad.

'That's fine,' he agreed.

44

'So that just leaves you with the cars, and the flowers. The presents for the bridesmaids and the best man. Oh! And the photographer,' Julie said with shining eyes. She was lost in a wedding mist.

Meany was lost too. Did other people go through this? Or did they just get a licence and get married? Cars, flowers, photographs? It was all a bit too much. But at least the photographs would be no problem. His friend, Sean, had a grand little camera. He usually took very good snaps.

'I forgot about the video. We must have a video,' Julie said suddenly.

'What for? We don't even have a television.' The minute the words were out of his mouth Meany knew he had said the wrong thing.

'Yes we do. I'll be bringing my telly and video from Dublin,' Julie said.

Meany's spirits lifted. One expense spared. He would enjoy watching television. It would save wasting money in Doyle's pub every night.

'Come on, let's make a cup of tea, then we can set a date,' Julie said.

Meany watched her moving about the kitchen. She was so graceful. Apart from her fancy ideas there was no lovelier girl than Julie. He was a very lucky man. The envy of every man in Doyle's. All the men in Wexford even. The whole country for that matter.

They chose the first Saturday in November for the wedding. At least, Julie did.

'I wish Mam was here to see me walk down the aisle,' Julie said wistfully.

'I wish my Mam could be here too.' Meany knew how she felt.

Julie hid her eyes from his gaze. If his Mam had been alive there would have been no wedding. One miser at a time was enough for her to cope with. But she was getting there. Meany was coming round. Slowly but surely.

CHAPTER SEVEN

Meany was glad that this would be Julie's last trip to Dublin. She would be away for about a month. He would miss her terribly. She phoned her boss to tell him that she was leaving. She promised to give him time to find someone else and offered to train them in. She also promised Meany that she would come home for at least two or three weekends during the month. She pleaded with him to go to Dublin. Her friends were throwing a farewell party for her. But Meany refused point-blank. This time Julie did not press him. She knew how much Meany hated leaving the farm. Besides, she'd had it all her own way so far. For the moment, enough was enough.

He and Julie had only argued once before she left. Meany did not see why he needed to buy a new suit. The one he had was fine. He had worn it less than a dozen times. Julie said it was old-fashioned. He didn't care, he was not into style. But Julie was. Now he would have two suits hanging in the wardrobe. What a waste. A new suit, shoes, shirt and tie, that was what she wanted.

At least he would be able to pick up a shirt and tie in the sales, he thought, as he swilled out the bucket. It looked like rain. If he was quick he would be able to get to the gas showrooms before they closed. He promised Julie that he would do that this week. She was getting impatient.

In the distance he could hear the sound of drilling. He stopped what he was doing and stared across the fields to the road above the farm. Two men, wearing what looked like headphones, were bent over their drills. Beside them was a huge stack of pipes. Meany's pulse began to race. Unless he was mistaken, they were gas pipes. He threw down the bucket and walked as fast as he could across the fields to find out.

*   *   *

The men stopped their drilling.

'My name is Freeney. That's my farm below,' Meany panted as he reached them. 'Are those gas pipes?'

'They are,' the taller of the two men replied.

'I was thinking of getting gas put in the house,' Meany told them.

The men nodded.

'It's a very expensive thing to do, isn't it?' Meany asked.

'That it is,' the shorter one agreed.

'Is there any way of . . . well, cutting down the cost?' Meany enquired.

'God, I don't know, do you, Jim?' The shorter man looked puzzled. 'By the way, he's Jim, I'm Tony.'

'I'm Meany.'

The two men smiled.

'Unusual name,' Jim remarked.

'Just a nickname,' Meany explained. 'So, do you have any ideas?'

Jim looked at his partner.

'Maybe we could help a bit. Work after hours. If you get my drift?' Jim said.

'You mean, do work on the side?' Meany asked.

'Work in our own time,' Jim corrected.

'And could you put heating in too?'

'Oh no! No, we don't do that. You'd be better off getting a local firm to do that kind of thing. We could run a pipe to the farm. That's all we would do,' Tony explained.

Meany thought for a moment. It might not be too expensive once the piping was done. 'What would you charge for that?'

Jim frowned. 'We'd need time to work it out. I'll tell you what, why don't you come back tomorrow and we'll give you a price.'

Next morning Meany almost ran up the hill. They were asking a third of the price he had been quoted. Meany tried to bargain with them, get them down even further. The men stuck to their price. The three of them shook hands on the deal and Tony promised that they would start work the following evening.

'You don't know where I could pick up a nice, cheap gas cooker, do you?' Meany asked.

'Not really. We're not from around here. Try the *Buy and Sell* magazine,' Jim suggested.

'I think you'd be better off advertising in the local paper,' Tony advised.

Meany thanked them for their advice and started back down the hill. The trouble was that Julie might read the paper and see his advertisement. No, there had to be another way.

*　　　*　　　*

Meany could barely wait until Friday. Julie would be home for the weekend. She would be thrilled to see the freshly dug trench. It already reached half-way to the farmhouse. The men were doing a good job. Just another few days and then the pipes would be laid. It has been easier than Meany thought. So far. But, what was not easy, was the thought of buying an engagement ring. It had been on his mind all week. He knew that he could not put it off any longer. Julie had said that she didn't really feel engaged without a ring. He would finish work early tomorrow, then go to the jewellers.

*   *   *

Meany stood at the counter and peered into the showcase. Rings and brooches, earrings and necklaces glittered back at him from their velvet boxes. Rubies, diamonds and emeralds studded the display. Meany looked at the price tickets but could not make them out. They must be in code, he decided.

'Sorry to keep you waiting,' the jeweller said. 'What can I do for you?'

'I want to buy an engagement ring,' Meany replied.

'Congratulations,' the man said shaking Meany's hand. 'We'll have to find something special for the lucky girl, won't we? What's her favourite stone? A diamond maybe, or a ruby? Does she like green? An emerald would be nice.'

Meany had no idea which stone Julie would prefer.

'How about this?' the jeweller asked as he placed a beautiful ruby ring on the counter.

'Its very nice,' Meany agreed. 'How much is it?'

The jeweller looked at the ticket and told him the price.

'Sir! Sir! Are you all right? Let me

get you a glass of water. Here, sit on this chair.' The jeweller dragged a chair from behind the counter.

'I'm OK,' Meany gasped. 'Overdoing it a bit, that's all.'

'You sure?' the owner of the shop asked.

'Yes, I'm fine now, thank you. Have you anything else, one with a different stone perhaps.'

'More or less expensive?' the jeweller asked, hiding a grin. He had seen men in shock before.

'Less,' Meany muttered.

One after the other the jeweller placed rings on the black velvet cloth. One after the other Meany turned them down. He had come in to buy a ring, not the shop.

The owner locked the showcase in front of them. With a sigh, he turned to the display shelves behind him. He chose a simple ring with no stones to hinder its design.

'What about this?' the jeweller asked, eyeing his watch.

Meany studied the silver circle with its rose shaped centre. 'That's nice,' he said. The price was nearer the mark too, under a hundred pounds. Thirty-four pounds to be exact.

'I like it,' Meany said. 'Yes, I like this one, don't you? I'll take it. Will you gift-wrap it for me?'

The jeweller nodded. He rubbed the ring with a soft duster. Then he wrapped it in tissue paper.

'Where's its velvet box? Meany asked.

'I'm afraid these rings don't come in boxes,' the jeweller explained.

'Why not?' Meany wanted to know.

He didn't half want jam on it, the jeweller thought. Poor girl. What a skinflint this fellow was. If he were getting engaged to the girl of his dreams, he'd be buying her a cracker of a ring.

'A box would cost almost as much as the ring,' the jeweller said pointedly. 'These rings are usually sold as … well, sort of funky rings. Fun jewellery. Mostly for young kids. Sometimes they buy one for themselves with their pocket money. Often with a pair of earrings to match.'

Colour flooded Meany's cheeks

'Are you saying that this isn't good enough for an engagement ring?'

'Well, as you're asking, it wouldn't be my choice,' the jeweller admitted.

'Maybe she wouldn't like it,' Meany worried aloud. 'Could we have a look at some of the others again, do you think?'

Meany left the shop with a gift-wrapped box clutched tightly in his hand. It had cost him ten times more than the first one he had picked. Julie should be very happy with her ring. He had spent an hour-and-a-half choosing it. He thought the jeweller could have been a bit more helpful. He seemed to be more interested in the time than making an important sale. And, as if he had not spent enough money, the man had tried to sell him two wedding rings as well. But Meany was not falling for that one. For a start, he did not need a wedding ring. Besides, what was the point of tying up even more money at this stage?

CHAPTER EIGHT

Meany listened for the sound of Julie's car. He had taken a lot of trouble to make everything look nice. He had washed the tablecloth and given it a rub with the old flat iron. A rabbit was stewing gently in a big cauldron on the stove. The owner of the bakery had given him a good price on yesterday's cakes. She'd thrown in a loaf of bread too. A few minutes in the side-oven would soon freshen it up again. He could hear the rustle of the box in his pocket as he moved towards the window. He leaned out and looked again at the line of the trench. It was up to the farmhouse now, ready to take the pipes.

*   *   *

Julie and Meany stood with their

arms around each other looking across the fields. She had really missed him these last couple of weeks.

'The pipe-layers have done well, haven't they?' she said with a smile.

'It didn't take too long after all, did it?' Meany replied. He felt no need to tell Julie the full story. 'Come on inside, you must be dying of thirst.'

Just in time, Julie stopped herself from flopping into Meany's chair. Once nipped, twice shy, she thought. She pulled out a hard kitchen chair instead and propped her elbows on the table.

'Something smells good,' she said as she sniffed the air.

'Rabbit. Paul Duggan was out hunting,' Meany said.

'Poaching, you mean.' Julie laughed.

'I gave him a stack of vegetable and potatoes in return.' Meany didn't want Julie to think he had got their supper for nothing.

'Any news while I've been gone?' asked Julie.

'Not that I've heard.'

'Did you get a chance to go and look at a cooker yet?'

'Not yet,' he replied.

'Ah, Meany!'

'I was too busy,' Meany said with a twinkle. 'I had to go to the jewellers.'

'Ooh!' Julie squealed.

'I suppose you'd like to see what I bought,' Meany teased.

'Yes please,' she admitted.

Meany watched as Julie ripped the paper off the little parcel.

'Oh Meany!' she said as she slipped the ring on her finger. It was a perfect fit. She waggled her finger so that the tiny stones glittered in the light. 'What an unusual ring.'

'Do you like it?' he asked anxiously.

Julie leaned forward and gave him a kiss. It certainly was different from any of the rings her friends wore.

The design was very pretty even if the stones were almost lost amongst the two white-gold hearts. 'It's so pretty Meany, really different.'

Meany beamed. The expense had been worth it after all.

All through the meal Julie turned her hand, this way and that. Letting the light catch the ruby chips.

'Are we going shopping tomorrow?' she asked as she finished the last of her rabbit.

'What for?' Meany paled.

'Well, they're almost ready to put the cooker in. They can't do it if we haven't got one, can they?'

'It will be a few days yet,' Meany said, playing for time.

'But they might not have one in stock. Anyway, I'll be doing the cooking so I should choose it.'

Meany could find no fault with her reasoning. But he tried anyway.

'I thought I'd look after that, as a sort of surprise for you.'

'That's really nice of you, but

honestly, I'd rather pick my own cooker. So it's decided. We'll go tomorrow morning.' Julie left her chair and sat on his knee.

Meany was no match for her loving arms and heady perfume. He was even deeper in trouble as she began kissing his ear.

'Tomorrow,' he murmured. He had lost again.

* * *

Julie was disappointed. The cooker she wanted was out of stock.

'It will be at least three months before we get another delivery,' the salesman told her.

Meany tried to hide his smile. She had picked the most expensive cooker in the showroom. 'Never mind, what about that one?' he asked pointing to a much smaller, cheaper model.

'Honestly. Trust you to pick the cheapest cooker in the place,' she snapped. 'It only has two rings. What use is that?'

'Why would you need more than that?'

'Because most gas cookers have four rings, that's why. I don't want any of the others, I want the one I chose.'

The salesman moved away and left them to argue it out. As he watched them a thought struck him.

'Excuse me, I wonder if you'd be interested in buying an almost new cooker? Identical to the one you chose.'

'No,' Julie said.

'Yes!' Meany replied.

'It's just that an American couple bought one last month. They have been called back to the States and rang to ask if we'd be willing to take it back. The woman said it's like new.'

*   *   *

Meany thought all his birthdays had come at once. He smiled at the pretty American woman. She wanted only half the amount she had paid for the cooker. Meany doubted if it had ever been used. Even Julie agreed that it was in perfect condition. But so too was the three seater settee with its matching easy-chairs. And the window seat with its roomy storage cupboards which would be ideal for them. They all looked brand new.

Meany felt a cold chill sweep through him. He had to get Julie out of this house before she found any more perfect buys.

'Come though to the dining-room, there might be something else that catches your eye.' The woman lead the way. Julie needed no second invitation.

'Oh look! That table and chairs would be just right for us, Meany,' she said. 'The chair seats match the rest of our furniture.'

Meany knew that they were a bargain but argued just the same. 'We have a perfectly good table and chairs already. They have been in the family for years,' he said.

'Exactly! Thank you, we'll take them,' Julie said decisively as she opened her bag and took out her cheque book.

'Now hang on a minute,' Meany objected. 'Where is all this money coming from?'

'The tables and chairs are my wedding present to you,' Julie said as she wrote the cheque. 'As for the rest, no doubt there'll be plenty of cash available when the sale of your land goes through.'

The colour of Meany's face changed from white to red then back again. How did Julie know about the sale?

He did not trust himself to speak until they were back in her car again. 'How do you know that I was thinking of selling the land?' he demanded.

'I didn't. I guessed. Everyone knows that developers are combing the area. They were seen driving along the road to your farm. After that they disappeared. A couple of weeks later they were seen coming out of Mark Austin's office. They looked very pleased with themselves. I put two and two together. Seemingly, I was right. Why didn't you tell me, Meany? What sort of marriage can we have if you keep secrets like that from me?' Julie's face was grim.

She had been in a bad mood all morning. Now Meany knew why.

'I wasn't keeping secrets from you,' he fibbed. 'So many things can go wrong with land sales. I thought it was better to wait until it was all signed and sealed, then surprise you. Not disappoint you.'

Julie's heart softened as she saw the hurt look on Meany's face. She felt terrible. There he was trying to give her a lovely surprise and she was busy attacking him.

'You are very thoughtful, Meany. I'm sorry I snapped at you,' Julie apologised. 'So, what price *did* they pay you?'

Meany subtracted thirty-thousand pounds from the true price.

'Wow!' That's brilliant,' Julie whistled.

'I suppose everyone knows about the sale now?' Meany asked.

'What difference? They'll know anyway once the bulldozers move in,' Julie replied with a frown.

'But they won't know the price, will they? You won't tell anybody, will you, Julie?' Meany fretted.

'Of course I won't,' Julie promised.

She glanced at Meany's worried face and wondered if she would ever really understand him.

CHAPTER NINE

For once in his life Meany didn't argue. Twenty pounds, not a penny less, was the price the pipe-layers wanted for connecting the cooker.

'And that's cheap. You know we don't usually do that kind of work,' Jim said.

'It's a special favour to you,' Tony added.

'And you'll take the old stove away?' Meany checked.

It almost broke his heart to watch his precious stove being smashed to pieces and dumped in the back of their truck. That gas cooker better be good, he thought, as he waved goodbye to the men.

*   *   *

When Meany came downstairs next morning a wave of longing hit him.

The new furniture was piled high in a corner. It was covered with sheets to keep it clean. The turf bucket was still in its usual place but the stove was gone, a stranger in its place. He picked up the gas wand and held it at arm's length in front of the gas jet. He turned the knob. Then he pressed the wand and waited for the explosion. But there was no explosion. Just a quick pop. A perfect ring of dancing flame appeared. At least the thing was working. He filled the kettle and placed it on top of the flames. They spread out all round it. Nervously, he turned the dial. The flames licking the sides of the kettle lowered magically. They burned brightly underneath it instead. Meany practised turning the jet up and down. Amazing. The flame did whatever you wanted it to do. He lit the other jets. He turned them on full, then lowered them. The cooker certainly worked, he'd give it that.

He turned the jets off. By then the kettle had boiled and Meany took it to the table. He poured the water into the teapot, then put the kettle back on the cooker. He frowned as he noticed the black marks on the metal grid. He would have to get rid of those before Julie saw them. He had not agreed to part with his old kettle. It was part of his life. Thick with grime from years of use. It had never been a problem before today. A sharp chisel should do away with most of that thick soot on its base. It would come up like new in no time. Meany placed another tick on the calendar. Just two more days before Julie would be home for good. It would be wonderful to be able to see her every day. No more lonely evenings. No more expensive phone calls with everybody in Doyle's pub listening to what he had to say. Chipping in. He and Julie would go for long walks at night. Spend less time at Doyle's. That would save money too. Not that he would say that to Julie. He'd just suggest that perhaps fresh air would be better than sitting in a stuffy pub. Julie liked to walk. As he made plans, Meany scrubbed the mud off the potatoes and put them on to boil. He aimed the wand at the gas jet. He was a dab hand at it now. But nothing happened. He pressed the wand again. Still nothing. He turned off the jet and tried the one next to it. Panic began to rise in his throat. He tried each of the jets in turn with the same result. Nothing. Silence.

'Why should this happen?' he asked himself.

The answer popped into his head almost at once. What a fool he was. The wand wasn't working. That was why the gas would not light.

'Matches. That's what I need, matches. Where are you hiding?' he muttered.

One after another he struck the little, red-tipped wooden sticks and held them towards the jets. There was still no sign of a flame. No hiss or gas.

Now what was he going to do? The pipe-layers were long gone. He could hardly ask the gas company for help. They might fine him, or worse. His panic spread. His legs shook and his hands trembled as he collapsed into his chair.

'Bloody spring!' he yelled as the broken coil attacked him. Julie was right, the chair was only fit for the dump. He would throw it out, get rid of it once and for all.

Too sore to sit down, Meany leant against the edge of the table and tried to think. There had been no sound from the cooker when he tried to light it. No hiss from the unlit jets. No smell of gas. No leak. That meant that the fault must be outside somewhere. A break in the pipes, perhaps. But where? Under the path behind the house? Meany hoped so. The pipes stretched all the way from the house along the full length of the field. Although the earth was newly dug it could take days to turn all that soil again. Three or four days perhaps. Julie would be home by then. The thought of that made him leap into action.

Meany cut a piece of bread and angrily scraped some jam on it. He would have liked a cup of tea but there was nowhere to boil the kettle. If only he still had the stove. If only he had not listened to Julie. But Meany was sensible enough to know that wishing would not solve his problem. Hard digging was the only way out. The sooner he got started with the spade the better.

The gravel behind the farmhouse flew and was mixed in with the freshly dug earth. He could rake that later. The important thing now was to keep going. By nightfall his hands were red and sore but he could find no sign of a leak.

All the pipes fitted neatly together

and there was not the slightest whiff of gas. He was glad that the trench was no wider or deeper. Even though the soil had been so recently dug, it was heavy from the rain. It was back-breaking work. Weary and sweat-soaked he gave up. He would set his alarm extra-early tomorrow and get a head start on the day.

At daybreak, and cursing the lack of a cooked breakfast, Meany trudged up the field. He picked up the spade which he had left as a marker and began digging. After three hours hard work, he hit the jackpot. He threw the spade aside and excitedly began removing the earth with his hands.

Only the circling birds heard his tortured cry as he uncovered the yellow gas cylinder buried deep in the ground.